Lola's

Rules for Friendship

For Pam, my forever friend
—J.M.

To Eddie
—S.P.

Balzer + Bray is an imprint of HarperCollins Publishers.

Lola's Rules for Friendship
Text copyright © 2017 by Jenna McCarthy
Illustrations copyright © 2017 by Sara Palacios

ISBN 978-0-06-225018-6

The artist used watercolor, colored pencils, cut paper, and digital media to create
the digital illustrations for this book.
Typography by Carla Weise
17 18 19 20 21 SCP 10 9 8 7 6 5 4 3 2 1
❖
First Edition

Lola's Rules for Friendship

written by Jenna McCarthy   illustrated by Sara Palacios

BALZER + BRAY
An Imprint of HarperCollinsPublishers

I know a lot about being a good friend.

I have at least 347 of them, and believe me, it's not by accident.

But we just moved to a new house, and the only kid I know here is my big sister, Charlotte.

And she doesn't exactly count.

My dad says strangers are just friends
you haven't met.
I look around my new neighborhood.
I have a *lot* of meeting to do.

Charlotte says I'll be lucky if I make one new friend.

"Are you kidding me?" Mom asks. "You're so good at making friends, you could write a book about it!"

Moms have some good ideas if you listen hard enough.

For starters, friends have lots of things in common.

I love lizards and licorice, and my favorite color is green.

No way! I love lizards and licorice too! But my favorite color is purple.

But not *everything* in common. That would be boring.

Friends also tell each other the truth.

You're the seventh nicest person I know!

Thanks?

This isn't always a good thing.

Friends know how to compromise.

"Let's play unicorns," says Stella.
"I want to paint!" Max says.
"Maybe we could paint unicorns?" I suggest.

You might have to get creative.

When you're feeling sad, a friend knows just what to do.

(Sometimes it takes a few tries.)

Friends offer to help without even being asked.

Um, Lola?
I don't think that's
a hat.

And they never tease you about it ...
unlike some sisters I know.

You can learn a lot of helpful things from your friends.

If I don't like something, I just put ketchup on it.

I'm going to try that with mustard!

Your mom won't always be happy about this.

To be a good friend, you have to be a good listener.

Someday I'm going to get a turtle and name her Myrtle. Or Marshmallow. Or Pistachio Or Fred . . .

It helps if you're patient.

Friends are always ready to share.

Want half of my
peanut butter and pickle
sandwich?

And they don't mind if you say "No, thanks."

Friends help each other solve problems.

"My mom says I can't play until I clean my room," Lily says.

"What are we waiting for then?" I shout. "Let's get some shovels and do this!"

After all, you can fit twice as many ideas in two heads.

Sometimes friends make mistakes,
but they always forgive each other.

Fake friends are easy to spot.

If you give me your
ice cream, I'll invite you to
my birthday party.

I think I'd rather
have the ice cream.

There are some things only a friend knows how to fix.

Every once in a while, friends might get in a fight.

trampoline

ice cream

swings

But they don't stay mad for long.

Without friends, life would be really boring.

Sometimes even a sister
can be a friend.

(Don't tell Charlotte I said that.)

But the coolest thing about friends?

They're just like flowers:
You can pick as many as you like.